Franklin and the Tooth Fairy

Franklin

Franklin is a trademark of Kids Can Press Ltd.

Text © 1995 Contextx Inc.
Illustrations © 1995 Brenda Clark Illustrator Inc.
Interior illustrations prepared with the assistance of Dimitrije Kostic.

Kids Can Press acknowledges the financial support of the Ontario
Arts Council, the Canada Council for the Arts and the Government
of Canada, through the BPIDP, for our publishing activity.

Published in Canada by
Kids Can Press Ltd.
25 Dockside Drive
Toronto, ON M5A 0B5

www.kidscanpress.com

The hardcover edition of this book is smyth sewn casebound.
The paperback edition of this book is limp sewn with a drawn-on cover.
Manufactured in Buji, Shenzhen, China, in 10/2010 by WKT Company

CM 95 0 9 8
CDN PA 95 20 19 18 17 16 15 14 13 12 11 10

Library and Archives Canada Cataloguing in Publication

Bourgeois, Paulette
     Franklin and the tooth fairy / Paulette Bourgeois, Brenda Clark.

ISBN 978-1-55453-734-1

1. Franklin (Fictitious character : Bourgeois) — Juvenile fiction.
I. Clark, Brenda II. Title.

PS8553.O85477F58 2011   jC813'.54   C2010-906681-2

Kids Can Press is a lorus™ Entertainment company

Franklin and the Tooth Fairy

Written by Paulette Bourgeois
Illustrated by Brenda Clark

Kids Can Press

FRANKLIN could count by twos and tie his shoes. He had lots of good friends, and one best friend, named Bear. Franklin and Bear were the same age. They lived in the same neighbourhood. They liked the same games. But one morning, Franklin discovered a way that he and Bear were different.

Waiting for the school bus, Bear put his paw in his mouth and wiggled a tooth back and forth. It jiggled and wiggled and then, with a tug, it came out.

"Look at this!" said Bear. "I lost my first tooth."

Franklin was startled. There was even a little blood on the tooth. "That's terrible. How are you going to tell your mother?"

Bear laughed.

"My teeth are supposed to fall out," said Bear. "It makes room for my grown-up teeth."

Franklin ran his tongue around his gums. They were smooth and firm … and completely toothless.

"I don't have any teeth," said Franklin.

It was Bear's turn to be surprised.

Franklin's friends shook their heads sadly. "Too bad," they said.

Franklin wondered why. He had never needed teeth before.

Bear wrapped his tooth in a bit of tissue and put it in his backpack. "I need to keep this safe," he said.

All the way to school, Franklin wondered why Bear
wanted to keep his old tooth. Especially if he was
going to get a brand-new grown-up tooth. Now *that*
was exciting.

"Why do you want to keep your tooth?" asked
Franklin. "Won't you get a big one soon?"

All his friends looked at him with amazement.

"Don't you know about the tooth fairy?" asked Fox.
Franklin shook his head.

"At night, before you go to sleep, you put your
baby tooth under your pillow. Then the tooth fairy
comes and takes the tooth away," explained Fox.

"But that's stealing," said Franklin. "Besides, what
does the tooth fairy do with all those teeth?"

There was a long pause.

Bear scratched his head. Fox swished his tail, and Rabbit twitched.

"I don't know," said Bear, "but she always leaves something behind."

"One of her own teeth?" asked Franklin.

Everybody laughed.

"Oh, Franklin!" said Fox. "The tooth fairy leaves a present."

Franklin wondered what kind of present a tooth fairy would leave.

"I hope I get some money," said Bear.

"When I lost my first tooth, I got a new book," said Raccoon.

"I got crayons," Fox said.

Franklin rubbed his gums. He wished he had a tooth to leave for the tooth fairy. He wanted a present, too.

Bear showed his tooth to Mr. Owl as soon as he got to school.

Mr. Owl was very excited. "Losing your baby teeth means you are growing up," he said.

Franklin did not say anything. He had no teeth, but he wanted to feel grown-up, too.

Franklin was quiet for the rest of the day.

Even at home, Franklin was quieter than usual.

"What's wrong?" asked Franklin's mother.

"I don't have any teeth," he answered.

"Neither do we," said his father. "That's the way turtles are."

"But I want teeth," said Franklin. His parents looked surprised.

"My friends get presents from the tooth fairy when they lose their teeth," said Franklin.

"Why do they get presents for old teeth?" asked Franklin's father.

"Because it means they are growing up," said Franklin.

"I see," said his father.

That night, just before bed, Franklin had a good idea. Perhaps tooth fairies did not know that turtles have no teeth. He found a tiny white rock to put under his shell.

He asked his mother to help him write a note. It read:

> *Dear Tooth Fairy,*
>
> *This is a turtle tooth. You may not have seen one before. Please leave a present.*
>
> > *Franklin*

Franklin woke up very early the next morning. He looked under his shell. The rock was gone, but there was a note instead of a present.

He ran to his parents' room. "What does it say?" he asked.

Franklin's father put on his reading glasses.

Dear Franklin,

Sorry. Turtles don't have teeth.
Good try.

Your friend, The Tooth Fairy

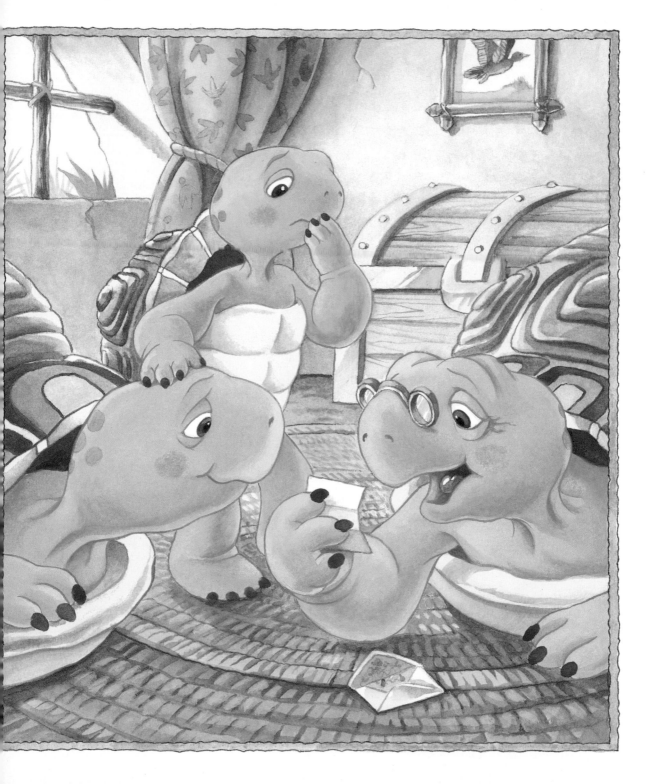

Franklin was very unhappy until he noticed a big wrapped package near his breakfast bowl.

"Open it," said Franklin's mother.

Inside was a beautiful book.

"Who is it from?" asked Franklin.

"From us," said his parents. "To celebrate your growing up."

Franklin stood very tall. "Thank you."

From then on, Franklin didn't worry about being different from Bear. He knew that, in all the important ways, he and Bear were exactly the same.